"*Unknowing, I Sin...* novella, imbued wi[...] grotesque. Highly recommended."
— Matthew M. Bartlett, author of *The Stay-Awake Men & Other Unstable Entities*

"Dread-inducing and memorable."
— Christi Nogle, author of *Beulah* and *The Best of Our Past, the Worst of Our Future*

"*Unknowing, I Sink* will drag you into a gelatinous pit of abject horror. The dread begins on page one and balloons until its shocking finale. With Huguenin's literary mastery and unapologetic weirdness, he's our Southern-fried Clive Barker."
— Nick Roberts, award-winning author of *The Exorcist's House* and *Anathema*

"A chilling inferno of the strange and unsettling. Huguenin's story quietly creeps while burrowing deep into your grey matter. . . . Small but mighty, [it] will blow your doors off."
— Brian James Lewis, *Damaged Skull Writer & Reviewer*

"One of the most literary horror books that I've picked up in the past year. . . . If you're looking for creeping horror with a satisfying twist and excellent writing, pick up *Unknowing, I Sink*."
— Daphne Strasert, *HorrorAddicts.net*

UNKNOWING, I SINK

a strange and horrifying novella

TIMOTHY G. HUGUENIN

First trade paperback and ebook editions of *Unknowing, I Sink* were published in 2020 by Independent Legions Publishing, with copyediting by Jess Landry.

ISBN-13: 978-0-9971474-5-2

This edition published in 2022
Cover design by Ben Baldwin
Author photo by Doug Stuart

For Dustin

∞

Julian stood on the cracked concrete path, chewing slowly on a leaf he had picked from a young sassafras growing in the high grass next to him. This was the first time he had seen Mr V's mansion, despite living fifteen minutes down the mountain. To a poor, small-town kid with not quite sixteen years of life experience and no driver's license to his name, the mildewing brick monstrosity before him was a wonder. Six Tuscan columns, taller than Julian's house down in the valley, seemed to function more as soldiers standing guard than weight-bearing pillars. The overhang they bore obscured the front door in its mid-morning shadow. A brass hawk's head glared over the entrance.

He didn't realize he was sweating until a breeze cooled his forehead. He wiped it with the back of his hand. His intestines felt jumbled.

First day of my first job, he thought. *Probably everyone feels this way.*

He looked over his shoulder down the long driveway, even though he knew his mom had already left.

A vision of next year: left hand on the wheel of his very own car, right hand on Stacey Cochran's thigh. Of course,

Stacey Cochran had never given Julian the time of day, and whatever second-hand rusty sedan he might be able to afford as a result of this job wasn't likely to impress her—but hey, it was his fantasy.

Okay, here we go. That car won't pay for itself.

He faced the house and forced himself up the steps. As he lifted his knuckles toward the door, an intercom crackled and made him jump.

"Did your father tell you my rule about cell phones?"

At first, Julian was too surprised to speak. After a couple seconds, he forced a nod.

"I mean it, son. If you so much as check it for the time, you'll be gone. I'm a private man, and I have no wish for any of my activities or possessions to be plastered up on social media for all the world to see."

He nodded again.

"Okay, come in. I'll unlock it."

He heard the deadbolt disengage. A quick glance up revealed a tiny camera tucked discreetly under the hook of the hawk's beak.

"If I was going to pay money for somebody to stand there and gape, I'd have bought another statue."

Julian looked down, ashamed at the impression he was making on his new boss. "Sorry, Mr V."

"Fine. Just open the door."

He entered. The high-ceilinged foyer was dimly lit by a dusty chandelier with only three working bulbs. A staircase led to the second-floor landing, shrouded by darkness. Cobwebs hung in corners and shuddered from the disturbance brought by the door's opening and closing. Curls of peeling floral-print wallpaper made him think of fingers beckoning.

Come; smell our roses. Smell our old garden's decay.

"Take the hall to your right."

Mr V's voice sounded from above. He looked up at the landing balcony, but he saw nobody.

2

"Well?"

Julian hustled down the hall.

"That next door on your left, that's where the cleaning supplies are."

The whole house must have been wired up with intercom speakers and cameras. Even in the utility closet (which was as big as his kitchen at home), Mr V continued to instruct him until he had gathered all the necessary materials.

"You'll start with the kitchen. Get it good enough to prepare lunch. After my meal, you can clean it more thoroughly."

Mr V got him started, but his direction lessened as Julian worked. After forty-five minutes, he hardly spoke. Julian took this as a good sign, that his work so far was pleasing enough that he didn't need to be micromanaged. As he scrubbed grease and rust off of the gas range's cast iron grates, he wondered if the relative silence meant he was no longer being watched. Had Mr V fallen asleep? Was he only checking the cameras once in a while to see Julian's progress? Or did he continue to look over him without comment? The thought of the old man silently leering at Julian's image on a screen was somehow worse than being constantly told how to execute minor tasks.

He stepped back from his work for a second and smeared his slick forearm across a heavy sweat that had gathered on his brow. Apparently, his employer didn't believe in air conditioning, even in the summer.

He reached into his pocket to check his cell phone, then thought better of it. Wasn't worth the risk that Mr V was still watching. This job was his only hope of making his dream of a new car come true—and maybe that would be enough to get a certain girl's attention...

After he set the grates all back in place, Mr V broke his silence.

"All right, good job so far. Noon approaches. I've always taken my meal early, so for me, it is already late. Not your

3

fault, of course. I neglected to tell you—and it seems the last person in my employ left the kitchen in greater disarray than I remembered. At least he stocked the fridge. I assume you know how to scramble eggs."

"Yes, sir."

"Very good. Prepare twelve. I will direct you to me when you finish."

Twelve eggs? Julian thought. *Has the dude not eaten since he fired the last guy?*

The refrigerator's contents supported Mr V's claim about his weird appetite: around six dozen eggs—and nothing else. Not even a bottle of ketchup.

He shrugged and cooked lunch. A drop of sweat fell into the food as he pushed it around in the pan. He froze, tried not to look guilty, waited for fifteen seconds or so. No reprimand came. He relaxed his shoulders and let out a relieved sigh.

Mr V led him down long hallways. Some were lit only by the sun coming through windows. Some halls had no windows, but here and there a weak bulb struggled against the dark.

That ugly floral print lined the walls, pink roses on what was probably a white backdrop at one time, now shades varying from cream to tan. Every so many feet, a gold-framed painting was dispersed. Some were portraits of various people Julian didn't recognize. Most were surrealist images. He let his eyes linger on these a little too long, trying to make sense of them, and they caused a strange feeling in his chest. Julian spotted a couple cameras along the way, but based on Mr V's comments, he believed there were many more hidden.

So, this is how weird you get if you become so old and rich?

He wondered if one day he would ever be as paranoid as this guy.

No way. This is another level.

Julian found himself standing in front of two large, dark wooden doors. Mahogany, he guessed—not because he knew anything about wood; it just sounded like something an old rich guy would want his big doors made from. Two brass rings hung where the doors met in the center.

"It's unlocked."

This time, Julian heard the voice from behind the doors as well as a speaker somewhere above him.

The ring was thick and heavy in his sweaty palm, and warmer than the plate of eggs in his other hand. He wondered why he had expected it to be cool, when the dark hall was so stuffy and humid. It was worse than the kitchen.

As the weighty door swung, a blast of even hotter air assaulted his face, and an astonishing brew of smells with it: flesh, wood, sweat, ink, paper, leather. A locker room full of ancient books.

Thick curtains stopped the sun from infiltrating tall windows. A gas fireplace blazed on the other side of the room. Innumerable book spines inhabited every other spare inch so that there was not a scrap of that ugly rose wallpaper to be seen. Instead of a vaulted ceiling that might better fit the old library's grand, mysterious character, above was a flat, white plane, upon which a dizzying number of images appeared. It took a couple seconds before Julian realized that they were live feeds from the cameras all over the mansion.

A smooth, white mound rested on a large table at the room's center. Adjacent to the table were a couple of computer towers and a projector, the cause of all that appeared above. This and the fireplace were the only light sources. Julian looked directly at the projector's bulb and instantly regretted it; what little he was able to see was now lost.

"Close the door, son. You're letting in all the cold air."

Due to his temporary blindness, he couldn't see Mr V, but this time he was sure that the man was in this room. He heaved the door shut and closed his eyes for a few seconds to readjust.

"Bring the food."

When Julian could again make out the thousands of books populating the shelves, he squinted at each shadowy corner of the room, careful now to avoid gazing directly at the projector. But Mr V seemed to be absent, or he was invisible.

"You still have a lot of work to do, and I'm very hungry."

His ears told him that Mr V was directly in front of him. Maybe the man was behind the table, hidden by that weird hump. He walked toward it slowly, holding a hand in front of his face to block the projector's light.

"That's it. Don't spill it now. I don't want you to have wasted the trip."

The body smell worsened as he neared. What had originally looked as a single, unidentifiable lump on the table became clearer. Not just one slick, shiny dome, it was connected to other... lumps? mounds? growths?

His groping mind latched onto these vague labels, desperate for comfort, for normalcy. Clarity, articulate truth, reality—his subconscious now found these as threatening. But even as his heart fluttered and his stomach clenched, he forced himself to believe that eyes could not deceive him from just two feet away.

The white hill on the table was not a decoration, a piece of equipment, or even a work of art, surreal as it was.

It was Mr V—or, more specifically, it was his naked, hairless belly. Mr V wore nothing but a small hand towel draped over his crotch. His legs and arms were remarkably skinny in relation to the prodigious gut. The head, from which a sunken pair of eyes gleamed back at Julian, was as bald and shining as the rest of the body.

Julian had seen plenty of fat men. But none in such an unexpected scene, none with skin so incredibly tight. And it wasn't just the nudity, or his hairlessness, or the terrible odor that made his throat constrict. It was this sense of the stomach's primacy. The arms, the legs—even, if possible, the head—all emanating from this great center, seemed so vestigial.

"Put it on top."

Julian started. In his shock, he had forgotten Mr V's personhood. The old man had become a science experiment, a great mammalian *something* grown on a petri dish. But Mr V's voice, at last attached to a face (but was it the face or this moist, white bulge that the voice belonged to?), jerked him from his stupor. He lifted the plate.

"Just the eggs, please. Take the plate back with you."

He paused and met Mr V's eyes, not sure he understood.

Mr V nodded. "Dump them on top of me. That's all I want. I don't need the plate or the fork. You may leave a napkin if you brought one, but it isn't necessary."

Julian did this, somehow managing to keep the eggs from spilling down the sides. He then stepped back, holding the plate in both hands between him and his boss.

"I realize," Mr V said, "the... *oddness* of my appearance." The egg pile bounced precariously as he spoke. "I imagine it is quite a shock. You see, I didn't know how to best prepare you for my... my *condition*... I'm an old man in need of help around the house, this much I told your father. That's certainly true, isn't it? The details about my condition—well, that's my own business, and it is hard to find decent help these days, *terribly* hard..."

He felt that Mr V expected him to fill this pause with some kind of acknowledgement. After a false start, he cleared his throat and took a breath. "Yeah," he said. "Yeah, I guess."

This satisfied Mr V, who nodded and continued speaking, much to Julian's dismay.

"There was a time that I was a lot like you, Julian. But you see now that I'm in no shape to get around. And yet, in a way, I do."

His eyes left Julian's and stared at the ceiling, where the images shifted. All the video feeds disappeared. A rushing mountain stream filled the absence. Dark green rhododendrons crowded its rocky bank. A trout lurked along

7

the current for its meal. The river's roar immersed Julian so that he forgot the books surrounding him and the odd, naked man on the table.

After a few seconds, the scene switched to night in a bustling, light-filled city. Julian had never seen a place with buildings so big and lit up. Some of the skyscrapers even flashed patterns up and down their incredible lengths. Buses and honking taxis shot by on streets that glowed yellow. People walked and chattered beneath bright, colorful billboards and neon signs with symbols that he could not understand.

Then the cityscape was gone, replaced by an endless field of golden wheat. He could almost feel the breeze that tickled and swayed the soft tufts. Long clouds in a gray sky brooded over the flat horizon.

"What a marvelous age we've been lucky enough to witness," Mr V whispered. "I can be anywhere, experience almost anything, right here, in the privacy and comfort of my own library. From Hong Kong, which you just saw, to Charleston, to this field in Kansas, to the red Australian outback. The internet is amazing."

The field transformed into something that looked a cross between an email inbox and Reddit. Where an inbox's messages would be were the words *My Groups* and a list of links and descriptions. He noticed a few with weird names like *alt.occult* and *alt.alienconspiracy*, but the website blinked away faster than Julian could read it all.

It was only when Mr V shut off the projector that Julian even bothered to wonder how he had controlled any of this in the first place. He turned to see if there was a remote or something in his hand, but the fire across the room turned Mr V into a black, dimensionless silhouette: a round slope topped by the eggs, a pagan monument marking the top of a treeless hill. The surrounding wall-to-wall bookshelves glowed orange. Dark, long shadow-fingers brushed the dusty books. For several seconds, the only sounds were the gas flame's steady, soft blowing, the computers' low whirr, and Mr V's slow breaths. Sweat rolled from Julian's temples, down the sides of his face, his neck, soaking his shirt. Mr V's stink had not abated. He tried breathing solely through his mouth, but that was worse—he could taste... he could taste *it*. He gagged, thinking about what *it* was that was in the air, in his lungs, on his tongue. He yearned to leave.

"Do you like books?" Mr V said at last.

"Uh, sure. Yeah."

"As you see, I have many. I don't read them anymore. I've read every book in this room more times than I can remember. I can quote any given page of any book in this room and tell you on which shelf it is located exactly." His silhouette grew a hand, and it flicked a dismissive wave. "I like to be surrounded by these books for their symbolic nature— and perhaps nostalgia—but I no longer am interested in their contents. There is so much knowledge on the internet. So many mysteries to solve, so many mysteries that *have* been solved already—and who knows this? There are deep, dark corners at the world wide web's end that few ever discover. There are—"

"Sorry, Mr V, but shouldn't I get back to work? I'm really sorry to interrupt you, but you got a big house, and..."

"Hm? Oh yes. My apologies. I'm afraid I did start to ramble on, didn't I? I rarely have company these days. Go on. Finish the kitchen, and I'll tell you what comes next."

"Okay. Yes, sir. Thank you."

He turned and took a couple steps for the door. He heard something—a whisper? A gasp?—and looked over his shoulder in case Mr V meant to speak again. The man said nothing. Julian doubled the length of his stride and leaned hard on the door.

Out in the hall, he wiped his wet t-shirt across his dripping cheeks and collected himself. The whole scenario was beyond strange, but it was the last few moments that he found the most puzzling. When he had looked back, he had seen Mr V's bare belly, the eggs gone. If they had fallen, why hadn't he asked him to replace them? Surely he could not have eaten the full dozen in those few seconds when Julian's back was turned. He shrugged and walked on.

After all that, it's the eggs *I'm worried about? That whole thing was a creep show.*

Immediately, he was ashamed for this thought. It was obvious the old man had some incredible sickness. The guy had to be so lonely and miserable, unable to get out and see anyone, nothing but his computer for company. Sure, he was fat and naked and liked the heat turned way up—but that was all likely attributable to what the man had referred to vaguely as his "condition," and not reasonable grounds for Julian's fear.

"Well, are you going to work for me, or aren't you?"

He jumped up and speed-walked for the kitchen. "Sorry! Yes, sir."

~

Julian never knew how clean a kitchen could be until he finally got Mr V to verbally sign off on his work, hours later. He could see his grimy face reflected in the shining floor. The stainless-steel range gleamed. The whole place smelled like citrus cleaning solution.

The dining room was next. Mr V made sure he didn't miss a single inch of the place, but at least it wasn't as greasy as the kitchen had been. Julian was willing to bet that the rest of the house didn't get much use. The worst thing he probably had to deal with from now on was dust. Maybe mold or something, if he was unlucky—but he figured Mr V would have to hire a professional if they came across that problem. He wondered if he would be able to keep this job long enough to fund that car he was dreaming of. The house was big, but it wasn't infinite. Would there be enough rooms to fill his summer with work?

A flicker in his mind: flame, shadow, a naked dome of flesh. His arm prickled. He wondered if he *wanted* to keep this up for a whole summer.

Just a lonely, diseased old guy. That's all. Nothing wrong with that. He's always cold because he's old and doesn't move around, so that's why he needs the fireplace turned up. And maybe he has, like, sensitive skin or something. Some people are allergic to cotton or wool or whatever, right? Doesn't mean he's a bad dude. He needs my help, and I need that car.It's a win-win.

His self-talk only marginally suppressed an ache in the back of his throat when he thought of returning to the library at his workday's end.

Just keep working, man. Just keep working.

~

Julian's pulse coursed through his ears as he paused in front of the library doors.

"Son, if I specifically ask you to come to the library, you don't need to wait for permission to enter when you arrive."

He wasn't waiting for permission; he was waiting for courage—but Mr V didn't need to know that.

New car, new car, new car, new car... With this inner mantra on loop, he entered Mr V's hot, rank living quarters.

"There you are, son. There you are."

Even though Julian knew what to expect this time, his eyes still did not naturally seek out Mr V's face. First, always first, was the belly, a psychic lodestone glowing white underneath its web browser sky. He focused all his will on meeting his boss's gaze and holding it.

"Would you like to be paid daily or weekly?"

"Uh, whatever. Daily, I guess. But whatever works best for you."

"Excellent. Daily suits me well. Weekly or bi-weekly payment schedules, in my opinion, don't allow the worker to feel the connection between wages and work accomplished. What is your cell phone number?"

As Julian relayed his digits, he watched them appear on the ceiling under the text *Send Money* and a dollar amount.

He did a double-take. It looked like Mr V was paying him five hundred dollars. He assumed he would be paid well, but he couldn't imagine that this was his *daily* wage.

"What, is it not enough?" Mr V said. "I know that I didn't discuss payment with you or your father. Perhaps a bit unusual, but I wanted to witness the quality of your work before I determined how much it was worth to me. But you did impress me. I admire a young man like yourself who is not afraid to get his hands a bit dirty, work up some sweat. Five hundred seems perfectly reasonable to me for today's work. Each day from now on, you will be paid a sum that I deem appropriate based directly on your work ethic as it either progresses, stagnates, or suffers."

Julian's mouth fell open slightly—but not for long, since the taste of sweat and skin soon touched his tongue and clamped his jaw shut.

"Does that arrangement suit you?"

"Yes, sir."

"All right, then."

The *Send Money* button blinked, and Julian felt his phone buzz in his pocket. He began to reach for it, then froze.

"Good catch," Mr V said. "Yes, even in the final moments of the workday, that phone of yours better not see the light outside your pocket. Remember my warning. I make no empty threats. If you touch that phone, you are gone. Leave it at home, from now on. Oh—and get here earlier."

~

"How was it?" Julian's dad asked.

"Good."

The Nissan's old struts creaked as they bounced down the pothole-strewn road between High Point and Augustus Valley. Julian stared out his window in a daze. Every couple seconds, he looked at his phone to prove to himself he hadn't seen wrong, hadn't misunderstood. Five hundred dollars for one day's work. He wasn't very good at math, but these calculations weren't difficult: in ten days, he would have five grand, assuming Mr V paid him the same each day. That's more than he had expected to get for the whole summer. He was getting a *cool* car, and not some ugly, rusted out, second-hand piece of junk, either. Nothing like his dad's Nissan, or his mom's Geo Tracker. Yeah, not anything remotely like that Tracker.

"Must have been *really* good."

"Huh?"

"The way you were just grinning there. Does Mr V have a granddaughter I don't know about or something?"

Julian saw his own goofy smile in the rearview and rubbed his face to regain control of it.

"Yeah—no, I mean. No, but he paid me, like, really good."

"Really? You know, I forgot to ask about that back when I called him. I figured it would be decent. He's got loads of cash. So what are we talking here?"

"Five hundred."

"For the week?"

"No, just for today."

They were both silent for a while. Then Julian's smile creeped back, and his dad laughed.

"Hell, maybe I oughta quit my job and go work for this guy. He got a position open for me too?"

Julian chuckled and checked his phone again. He didn't have Stacey's number, but they were Facebook friends, so he opened the Messenger app.

New car! he typed. He hesitated, then added, **Wanna ride?**

Service was spotty on this mountain, but within a minute, he saw that the message had gone through. In twenty more seconds, Stacey had seen it. His heart stuttered when he saw that she was composing a reply.

They hit a dead zone, and he cursed this valley.

"You know what, Jules?"

"Yeah?"

"I know you're thinking you could go out and buy something in a couple days. But I just wanna tell you, even if you are sure you'll be getting enough for payments, it's always better if you pay the whole thing in cash. Especially if you are getting your cash saved up pretty fast. You'll end up paying much more in the end if you stretch it out."

He hardly heard his dad. His eyes were stuck on his phone, watching to see when his service would come back. At last, Stacey's reply came in:

How do I know you again?

He frowned. His high school wasn't that big, and she was only one year ahead of him. They shared the same PE class, for crying out loud!

School. I'm in your PE class?

The seconds before her reply were unbearable.

LOL.

Ouch. Maybe scoring a date with Stacey would take a little more than any old vehicle. Independent mobility alone wouldn't impress her. She had her own, after all: a lime green, cloth-top Jeep Wrangler.

Something flashy, something sporty. That's what he needed. Something *fast*. Something Stacey Cochran couldn't say no to.

∞

Over the next few days, Julian put increasing amounts of elbow grease into his work. (*Elbow grease* was an Old Guy Word, one his dad always used. Considering the man he was working for, he figured that using an Old Guy Word was appropriate.) He made sure to leave his phone at home. He leaned hard on any surface that required a stiff scrubbing, to the point that his arms were sore by the day's end. He avoided lingering after he had been summoned to the library—and not only because of the smell and the temperature. As soon as he set Mr V's meal on that altar of a stomach, he turned on his heels and got back to work without conversation. He wanted his boss to know that he was there for *work*, dammit, and *hard* work, not idle chatter (there was another Old Guy Word). But as zealous as he tried to appear, his pay steadily decreased. He could feel his dream of impressing Stacey slipping away, and fast. On Thursday, when Mr V stated his compensation would be at a new low of $175, he decided to speak up.

"Mr V, could I ask you something?" He meant to speak calmly, but he blurted it quickly, before Mr V could send the money. He chided himself for sounding desperate and whiny.

Mr V's eyebrows lifted, and the corners of his lips raised slightly. "Of course, son. And here I thought you had grown sick of me."

Julian took a breath, and held it. Maybe it wasn't effort alone that his boss really wanted. The guy was lonely and diseased. Julian's was the only face he saw. He thought back to the first day, feeling trapped here in this stifling library as Mr V droned on about the internet and books and whatever.

"Well? What's on your mind, son?"

Maybe what Mr V really wanted was somebody to talk to. No—somebody to *mentor*.

"I, uh," Julian said, sucking back the question about his payment and trying to think of how to replace it. "I was wondering, like, if you could tell me more about one of these books."

Mr V's smile opened and bared his teeth—what was left of them. Apparently, he hadn't even left home for a dentist in a long time.

He's old, he reminded himself, ashamed at how quick he was to judge Mr V. *Sick. Not lazy.*

"You like the books? Good for you! Good for you!" His belly bounced in his delight. "Too many kids these days think reading is for losers. Couldn't be further from the truth. For a little while, I admit, I wondered if you were among that sad, ignorant class of children. But I'm happy to see I was wrong."

He looked to his side, half rolled for a better view, and lifted a hand to point at a book. The effort seemed to strain him heavily, and Julian rushed to the shelf.

"No, no, the yellow one. Well, I suppose it's not as yellow as it once was... There you go."

Julian wiped a mess of cobwebs and dust from the top of its browning pages. The clothbound spine was threadbare along its edges, and the title was long gone, if it had ever appeared anywhere on the cover. He did not open it. He felt that one wrong move and the thing would crumble to powder in his hands.

Mr V had settled back into his default position. He sighed and closed his eyes. A drop of sweat slipped down from his brow as he took four deep breaths. When he had recovered himself, he looked at Julian and raised his eyebrows.

"Well, son, open it. It's not just for decoration—well, it shouldn't be. Like I said, I have memorized every word of it, and I have no way to reach them, besides. The internet—oh, there I go again. Read it, read it!"

He lifted the front cover slowly. It resisted at first, having been shut for decades. But Mr V would not have him hesitate for too long. He winced when he heard a soft crack upon fully opening it. Mr V remained enthusiastic and showed no sign of concern. Julian inspected the title page.

Phänomenologie des Geistes

—

Ge. Wilh. Fr. Hegel

To Julian's dismay—no, to his *relief*—the book was obviously unreadable. Mr V's smile turned to a frown, then he closed his eyes.

"Of course. My mistake, my mistake, my mistake. I suppose you wouldn't be very fluent in German at your age. Public schools. Shelve that one; I'm sorry. But soon enough! Soon enough. You will see. Our minds are not as limited as you have been led to believe. Should you wish to read that book, I will help you." He paused. "I don't suppose your French is very good?"

"No, sir."

"Understandable. Not your fault. Keep Jean-Baptiste Lamarck in mind for when you become proficient."

"Uh-huh. Sure."

"Okay, for now, we'll find something from not so far away, shall we? And perhaps something a little... well... exciting. Something a young man like yourself is sure to love. Yes... the shelf above the Hegel, yes, now follow that to the corner—okay, now three more over on the next wall—yes, there you go."

This book's gray dust jacket was torn in some spots, and the ink had rubbed off in places, but as a whole, the book was in better shape than the last one. He brushed away the dust. The title, printed in curvy, funky, yellow cursive, seemed familiar:

Do Androids
Dream
of
Electric
Sheep
?

The upper right corner, in white:

Phillip K. Dick

"Perhaps this choice surprises you," said Mr V. "Yet I find that sometimes fiction can convey truth even better than nonfiction. Of course, it depends on the author. Oh my, I'm sorry. You've read this one already, right?"

"No, sir. No, I actually..." He was going to say *I haven't heard of it before,* but he remembered his goal of winning back his original, ridiculous salary. It might be a bad idea to bum Mr V out. So, he finished, "...I had been meaning to, just haven't gotten around to it."

"Wonderful, wonderful. Now, you take that home, and don't you dare bring it back until you have finished it."

Julian nodded.

Great, he thought. *More homework. Though I guess the title sounds kinda cool.*

"Well, then," Mr V said, looking up at one of the camera feeds. "Your father's here already. How time flies. Okay, don't stay up too late reading! See you in the morning."

Julian tucked the book under his arm. He still hadn't been paid, but he wasn't sure whether or not he was supposed to bring it up. Fortunately, Mr V noticed his hesitation and remembered.

"Of course, of course. Speaking of books gets me... I lose track of things."

The payment screen was still projected above. Mr V glared at it. The first digit switched from a *1* to a *5*. The *Send Money* button blinked.

Julian looked at the floor. He hadn't expected this to work as well as it had. He dared not show too much emotion. Where did the line fall between gratitude and greed?

"Thank you, Mr V," he said as nonchalantly and humbly as possible.

"Quite welcome, young man. You impressed me today. It should be rewarded. Oh, one more thing—how are we on eggs?"

"We, uh..." Julian closed his eyes, trying to envision what was left in the fridge, but all he saw was the inverse of the display above them, a bright *$575.00* stamped on his brain.

Get a hold of yourself, man.

"I think we should be good for a few more days."

"Wonderful. We shall restock on Monday. I'll remind you on Saturday that I want you to bring them in. If you don't mind. I'll reimburse you, plus extra."

"Yeah, no problem."

"Excellent. See you tomorrow morning."

"Sure thing. You too."

Julian didn't realize he had grown used to the stench until he sucked in some of the hall's relatively fresh and cool air. The wallpaper's roses seemed a brighter, more welcoming pink than before.

Though the library's heavy doors were shut behind him, he could still feel the weight of Mr V's gaze. As he walked, he imagined the man lying naked in that stifling room, peering at the ceiling, following him across each camera's feed, all the way to the front door. Did those cameras show the tremble in his hand as he reached for the handle? Did he step outside too quickly? Too slowly?

He likes me, he reminded himself. *Gotta chill out. So I have to read a few dumb books on the side. Big deal.*

~

"Oooh, what's *that*?"

Carmen, Julian's little sister, bounced around him and grasped for the book. He twisted away.

"Nothing, it's for big people."

A fat lower lip shot out. "I am a big person! I'm seven now!"

Julian chuckled and tussled her hair. "Maybe later, all right?"

He tried to hurry to his room without looking too suspicious. Finally alone, he locked his door and took a closer look at the book. It was hard to make out details in the library, even with the projector on, and he had kept it tucked tightly under his arm on the ride home, not wanting to draw any attention to it. He didn't know why he felt the compulsion to hide it. His dad was always bugging him to lay off the video games and read a little more, so he probably would have been proud. Maybe it was that no matter how often he told himself he shouldn't fear the old man, he couldn't yet shake that mansion's aura of malaise. It was like the library had contaminated this book with its spores so that he felt wrong keeping it on his person.

Or, more likely, he didn't want his dad pestering him about it.

Maybe a bit of both. And—most definitely—he needed to admit to himself that he had an irrational fear of old people.

Naked old people. One in particular, who ate nothing but twelve eggs every day before noon; who never left his bed (table!), not even to urinate, as far as Julian could tell; who had a mountain for a midsection—

Who is sick, who is lonely, who needs someone who talk to more than a clean house he'll never use...

A dismembered sheep was displayed on the dust jacket. Not gory, just... deconstructed. A head in one box, the wooly torso in another, four legs with their own boxes beneath the head. Transistors and a diagram for what Julian figured must be a robotic sheep or a radio... or... well, maybe he would read a few pages, to see what this was all about...

But it had been about a month since school let out. His eyes glazed over, unaccustomed to traversing paths across printed text. Though he turned two pages, he didn't absorb anything. His mother called him for dinner.

I'll try again later. Gotta get through at least some, in case Mr V asks.

His family had a No Phones At The Table rule, so before leaving his room, he sent a quick message to Stacey, a GIF of a Ferrari speeding down an empty highway. He had to send her *something*, even if it was dumb. Just get her used to him.

"Booger? It's getting cold!"

"Just a minute. And don't call me that anymore! I'm not a little kid."

He thirsted for a reply—anything, even something mean or sarcastic or... or... well, *anything*. He wondered if this is what his dad felt like when he opened his pack of cigarettes to find out that there was only one left when he needed two.

"Not just a minute!"

Still no reply, nor indication she had seen it. He sighed, tossed his phone on his pillow, and ran to the dinner table.

∞

Friday morning dragged slowly. Stacey still had not said anything, and his soul withered with every second he spent in Mr V's house—every second without his phone. It was good that he had left it at home, because he didn't think he could have resisted.

As he mopped the balcony in the foyer, he examined a painting at the top of the stairway. Now that he had met Mr V, he recognized its subject. A younger, healthier man—but the eyes were the dead giveaway: the all-consuming glare. Their life-like intensity was staggering, blazing with a sublime confidence, unbridled intelligence, ferocious hunger for excellence. Julian felt that these traits, though likely tempered by age and infirmity, still smoldered within the man in the library. The work was a testament not just to Mr V but also to the artist's skill in communicating, with so few square inches of paint, the essential spark of a great man.

Julian stared down a stretch of hall that he had not inspected before. Again, he spotted only a couple cameras, but he knew there were more hidden in the shadows. The same decaying floral wallpaper wrapped the interior, though the window drapes stole most of the light and color so that the roses appeared nearly black. His pulse quickened as his eyes fell on a long, dark figure in the far corner.

"Hey!" He brandished the mop handle in what he hoped was a threatening manner. "I see you there! Who are you?"

The man-like figure didn't move. A low chuckle came from it.

His reflexive fear gave way to embarrassment as he considered the situation. Even if Mr V had left the front door unlocked after Julian entered this morning, there was no way that an intruder would have gone unnoticed by Mr V's omniscient surveillance. This must be another decoration.

"Well, come on, then. Meet my friend." The voice was now clearly Mr V's, coming from a speaker above the shape. Julian's ears burned as he leaned the mop against the wall and then approached the mysterious form.

It was a terra cotta statue. An armored man with a feathered hat presented a bowl in both hands.

"Julian, meet Juan Ponce de León, an ancestor of mine— so my great-aunt would have us believe, though I have not been able to obtain sufficient verifiable evidence of the lineage she supposedly traced to him. Of course you know that he was a conquistador. Ordered by the Spanish government on an expedition to find the fabled Fountain of Youth. Here, he gifts to you a sip of the nectar in his vessel. Drink from it, and taste everlasting life."

Julian was surprised to see that there was, in fact, liquid in the bowl presented to him. He wondered if its charcoal hue was due to the lack of direct light, or if there was a dangerous mold growing in the earthenware. Surely, it was only water in there.

Silence leaned heavy on him. He didn't know if he was supposed to fill it. Maybe Mr V was allowing him time to admire the statue. The dimness required him to bring his face extremely close to inspect it. Intricate details were etched into the sculpture, tiny designs on the breastplate, stitches in the sleeves. Incredible attention had gone into the pointed goatee's coarse, stringy texture. So why had the sculptor left the eyes so blank, without so much as a circle etched in to indicate an iris or a pupil?

He found himself caught in the statue's vacant stare. An ache grew in the center of his chest—tiny, an icy pinprick inside his heart... he was... it seemed...

"*Drink.*"

The word drifted to Julian's ears, lower than Mr V's chuckle before, so low that he wondered if the old man had only whispered it by accident.

Doesn't look so bad, he told himself. *It's just water.*

He bent his head, grasping the statue's clay hands beneath to steady himself. His fingertips slipped over wormy veins, silk-smooth. The bowl smelled like mildew.

Julian closed his eyes and took a breath.

"Good Lord, son, what are you doing? I didn't mean it *literally*. Come on, now, it's time for you to whip me up some eggs."

His sharp exhale splashed the water over the bowl's lip. Eyes bugging in incredulity at what he had almost done, he took one last look at the soldier's face. One side had been weathered into obscurity, a graven image devolving into its formless source. How had he not noticed?

~

"Take a seat over by the fire."

Mr V had muted the projector after Julian arranged the usual mess of scrambled eggs on top of the white altar— Julian noticed that he only took his lunch in the fiery dark— but he made out a shape near the hearth: a low-centered hulk curving up to pointed corners, a winged demon crouched close to flames so it might remember home.

Without paranoid imagination: a large wingback chair facing the fireplace.

Julian circled the room, feeling along the bookshelves to guide his way rather than passing straight across and coming too close to Mr V. He wrestled the bulky chair toward the table. He wished rather to stare into the fire, but he knew his mentor required an attentive pupil.

He compromised—with the chair's back to the fire, he could still point the front toward the corner of the room, with Mr V just on the edge of his sight. But when he did next glimpse the man, his eyes locked on to the body.

The eggs were gone. It had been seconds—a minute, *maybe*—since he had turned away. He scanned the floor. It was too dark to know for sure, but he didn't think they had slipped off. For one thing, Mr V hadn't asked him to clean them and cook more.

Julian racked his memory. Had Mr V been eating as he made his way to the fireplace? It was true that he hadn't exactly been watching—the opposite, really. But it was also true that he had never actually *seen* Mr V consume his daily ration.

And how in the world could a sick man, who got winded by leaning up and pointing to a book across the room, possibly have eaten an entire dozen eggs in less than a minute?

Dude, who cares? He's an old slob, and he slurps scrambled eggs like a vacuum. Why is this even a thing I'm worrying about?

It was bizarre to contemplate, but it niggled at his growing unease nonetheless.

"Have you considered the stars, Julian?"

Before he could even interpret the question, brilliant white grains dusted the now purplish-black ceiling. They swirled, realigned, shifted, so that he became nauseous.

"The vastness of it all. Seemingly infinite—surely beyond our current ability to comprehend—even our own *galaxy*— yet what is truly infinite? There are limits to the universe. So science tells us even now. We shall continue to find, to explore—to stretch, if you can believe it, along with the universe. But that's what it's all about, isn't it? Finding the limits. Then *stretching* them. Even the most microscopic advance is a step to the next stage."

"I, uh... I guess? I mean, I don't know much about astronomy."

The stars froze, to Julian's incredible relief. He focused on his breathing. Though the stars had stopped moving, he felt like the room had continued to spin underneath the calm, silent sky. The fire's heat exacerbated his discomfort. He wiped slick bangs from his eyes.

"I mean to teach you a universal principle. Of perceived limits. Not just about the universe, in the macro sense. It is easy to say such and such about something so big and, to put it clumsily, so *far off* as the universe. In view of such incomprehensible grandeur, we divorce ourselves from it, think we are apart from it. Immune to it. So we do not feel so small. But we cannot escape it. We are the micro in the macro."

The room had stopped spinning, but this lecture was not helping. Did this have something to do with that book? He now wished he had tried harder to read it. But he had the feeling it wouldn't have helped. As Mr V himself had admitted, the man tended to ramble. Julian did his best to remain present. If it was obvious that he wasn't paying attention, he might not make the money he was counting on. Maybe he would learn something.

"I'm afraid I'm doing a poor job of explaining myself. Of course, the truths I've unveiled did not find me all at once. It was a process." He laughed softly, as if he had said something witty. Julian missed the joke. "Everything's a process. One step at a time, even if some steps are micro of the micro. Microbehood!" He laughed again.

Even if he couldn't find the humor, here was something Julian could wrap his head around. Gradual change. One step at a time. Like saving up for a car.

"I assume you have not made it very far in your studies."

It took several seconds before he realized his boss was referring to *Do Androids Dream of Electric Sheep?*.

"Oh, sorry. I, uh, I started it, but no, I, uh... I got distracted."

Mr V nodded. Something beneath the table moved. Something snake-like.

Julian squinted. It was a cable or cord or something, presumably having something to do with the computer/ projection setup. It must have shaken loose from whatever had secured it to the table. Now it hung loose in a slack U below, as if it were trying to mirror the greater shape above it.

"Keep trying. You'll get there. Philip K. Dick can be difficult, even to those accustomed to mind-stretching. This one is not his most challenging novel. Micro-stretches toward your macro-future. Got it?"

"Yeah. Sure. I'll definitely get through the first chapter tonight."

"Excellent! Now, about your continued employment."

Julian's breath hitched.

"Don't be alarmed. I have been greatly impressed with you this week. And I'm no fool. As big as this house may appear to someone like you, you'll have every nook spotless before we both know it. You've already made more progress in a single week than I had expected. The seemingly infinite reveals its limits, right? But again I would like to stretch that. Of course I want you to finish cleaning through the house's entirety. Your answer to what I'm about to propose will not affect that opportunity."

"Okay."

"So, after you finish your original job—which will be soon, I now believe—I will still need someone around. Someone to prepare meals, go to the store, this and that. And you will have exclusive access to the library—under my supervision, of course."

Julian could hardly believe his luck. He had already been wondering how he might stretch this job out long enough to ensure his ability to afford a vehicle worthy of Stacey's attention. Now the problem was solved. He was going to be the richest teenager in southern West Virginia.

"Mr V, I would love to."

"Are you sure, now? Payment will still work the same. It may increase, but it also may decrease. Each day, your reward will be judged to be according to your effort. And I am the judge."

"No problem, sir. I'm sure we won't have any issues."

"Excellent, excellent. No, I don't expect we will, not if you keep it up. I've been pleased. You're nice to have around, son. And you're not like some of the other kids who have failed me. You work hard; you can follow instruction. You'd be surprised how many are unable to keep even the simplest of my rules."

"Yeah," Julian said, shaking his head. "Kids these days, right?"

Mr V chuckled. "You amuse me, son. I like you. I so hope you will not take advantage of my favor. I have little reason to believe you will. But I have lived a long time and have known many people. Unfortunately, my experience has taught me to trust only myself, in general. Yet there are some who surprise me."

~

Back to work upstairs, Julian wondered how long he had been in the library. There were no working clocks that he had found, and as his phone was at home, he only had a general sense of time based on how the sun appeared through the windows. It felt much later than it should.

Of course, Mr V had kept him longer than previous lunches. After telling Julian he liked him, he went on again about work ethic and curiosity and all that weird mumbo-jumbo about *stretching*, whatever that was supposed to mean. Julian had lost track. His head still hurt from trying to follow it all.

It wasn't that what Mr V said was *always* dull. It was just that the man would say one thing that he could barely understand, and as he was chewing on that, the monologue sped away into metaphors and higher concepts and philosophies that lost him completely. He was surprised that he actually *wanted* to follow Mr V's train of thought, as he never before had been very interested in his classes at school. But Mr V's train was just too damn fast.

One step at a time, like he said. Stretching my mind, one step at a time. Like saving up for the car. Like cleaning this humongous house.

He was now in a room that reminded him a bit of the library, as there were bookshelves built into most of the walls. But there were more windows in this room, and the curtains were pulled back to let in the sun. A telescope was in the corner, angled skyward. Next to it stood another conquistador statue. Julian's heart had skipped when he first saw it. It looked the same as the other one, except for its pose: arms at its sides, sans bowl. An old desk was in another corner, on which maps and star charts were haphazardly layered, along with a few pencils and measuring tools. For some reason, the walls lacked that horrible rose print wallpaper. The air smelled fresher, even though it was still quite warm.

He pretended he was dusting the desk and surrounding area more thoroughly so that he could get a better look at the charts. They were so fascinating, these artifacts of a pre-digital world he would never understand.

He did not pay attention to his hands until his wrist knocked into a glass paperweight. He tried to catch it, but it was too late. The shattering sound seemed to last longer than it took for its fragments to shoot across the floor and come to rest. Each tiny amber shard, irrevocably divorced from its former whole, was now its own smaller, individual unit. Its shape and position from the epicenter were the only clues to what each piece had once been. The sunlight glowed in them, and they looked as wet as rain droplets. They might have been beautiful to someone less worried about keeping a job. To Julian, it was a disastrous new galaxy representative of his lost hopes.

"Mr V, I'm so sorry. I don't know how this happened. I really didn't mean it."

"What are you talking about?"

Julian looked up at the only camera he could find. It looked no different from any of the rest. Maybe a little older. But there wasn't any sign of it being broken.

"Come on now, don't leave me in the dark. Hey, where are you? I'm afraid I was dozing and lost track of your position."

"I'm in this room with the telescope."

"Oh, of course, of course. Yes, there you are. Well."

Mr V paused; Julian braced himself.

"Okay, okay, don't, uh... I'm sure everything will be okay. Just, uh... just take care of... just make sure it's all cleaned up, and, uh..."

Mr V's voice trailed off. Julian wondered if there was something wrong with the camera's signal. If there was, it was obvious that Mr V wished to hide it. It sounded like he wasn't too concerned about the accident.

He was curious about this new possibility. "Was it expensive?"

"That old thing? Uh... no, I'm sure... don't worry. It's not like I use it these days. Just, you know. Take care of it."

That didn't really tell him much, but Mr V's cagey tone supported his suspicion and gave him the boldness to try something much riskier.

Slowly, he raised the feather duster above his head. He held it there, waiting for some comment about this absurd behavior.

Silence.

With his other hand, he pressed his thumb against his nose.

"Mr V?"

"Yes?"

Julian smiled. The camera didn't work. He lowered his

arms, relaxed his shoulders, closed his eyes. Took a deep breath.

"Nothing. Never mind. I got it all taken care of."

"Excellent. Let me know if you need anything further. Any special cleaning solution, you know. To get out stains, or what have you."

"I'll let you know."

As he swept up the glass, he felt incredibly light. He couldn't stop smiling from this newfound sense of privacy, limited as it was.

It was funny, now that he thought of it, how scared he had been, for nothing. All the man seemed to care about was twelve scrambled eggs a day, a good internet connection, and having someone around to dump his knowledge on. Of course, there was his obsession with watching over Julian as he worked, and that weird quirk he had about cell phones. But the dread that had filled Julian had no rational basis. Maybe Mr V wasn't all that bad.

Just as he was thinking this, the statue caught his eye again. A chill crawled up his back, like a spider with too many legs. He shuddered.

∞

"I have a question for you."

Julian snapped his attention back to Mr V. His mouth was dry, and his chair's generously cushioned back was wet with his sweat. His lethargic mind strained to recall what his boss had been talking about. He couldn't even pick up on some context to avoid responding like the idiot he probably was.

No, he couldn't remember—not just Mr V's words, but even *getting there*.

Must be near the end of the day. But when did he call me back to the library?

The rooms he had cleaned after lunch all blurred in his mind.

There was the room with the telescope and star charts— that one took a while, since it was so big and because he didn't feel as keen on leaving the one place where he knew he wasn't spied on. Some more work in the hallway—easy stuff. Sweeping, mopping, and dusting the frames of portraits and a few sculptures. He couldn't recall any details, but there probably weren't any worth remembering. Some other bedrooms, maybe? Maybe there was a bathroom? When had

Mr V told him to stop working? Strange that all of this was so elusive. He felt like he was coming out of a trance. Mr V's manner of speaking sometimes took on a nearly hypnotic rhythm and tone that reminded Julian of a magician, maybe, or some preachers he had heard on the radio.

"Remind me of your age, son."

"Fifteen," he said. He was relieved at a question he could answer with confidence. "I'm turning sixteen a week from tomorrow."

"What do they teach you in school regarding history? I don't mean in the broad sense—western civilization, American revolutionary, et cetera, et cetera." He waved his hand. "Of course, all that is important. I mean more... well... more locally."

Julian took a moment. His lethargy was wearing off. He still couldn't remember too much since lunch, or how he got there, but at least he felt more connected to himself.

"Yeah. Um, in third grade we all get taught West Virginia history. Since then, not much. I don't really remember."

Mr V nodded. Below the table, he saw that snake-like cable whip.

"Of course, of course. I am glad they teach this, though I wish they would revisit the subject later on, when a youth has a better ability to find his identity within our state's ongoing story. I do not blame you for forgetting things that you likely found difficult to synthesize at that age. This is the problem of all failing history curricula—you are taught dates and disconnected *facts*; you aren't told the *story* connecting them, or—most importantly—connecting *you*. But what I mean to get at now is even closer to you than what you learn in school. I'm talking about the history of this area. It is extraordinary. What do you know about your hometown?"

"Augustus Valley? I, uh... I mean... I guess it was a mining hub back in the day, right?"

"Yes, yes. The biggest in the state. Very important. But that's not what I mean."

"Okay... Well, not much happens there nowadays."

Mr V sighed. "They have told you nothing. I should have known. Indeed, it is likely they know nothing themselves. Very few people appear to remember. To *see*. Even to me, it is perplexing."

Julian couldn't fathom Mr V's interest in the valley. There was nothing special about it. Just another small town in West Virginia on its deathbed.

"There have been... anomalies, for lack of a better word. All throughout Augustus Valley's history—a mere blip in the grand macro timeline that is the History of the Universe. Yet... I wonder what strange stories could have been told, had there been a witness prior to our species settling in this mysterious locale."

Julian almost asked what he meant, but he wasn't sure how stupid that would make him look. Of course, just sitting there with his confusion plainly painted on his face didn't help.

Mr V continued, "Did you know that there have been several mass disappearances in your town?"

"People leave, like, all the time. Maybe they just moved away?"

"No, that's not what I am talking about. I mean scores of people, one day they are there, the next day—vanished. No obituaries. No records at all of their deaths, other than the plain *absence* of their persons. In some cases, hypotheses are proposed as to the cause. In *some* cases."

Houston, we're getting some crazy-vibes. This guy has been staring at his giant screen too long.

"I can see that you don't believe me. But you admit to knowing nothing about your own hometown. While I, on the other hand, am very familiar with it. I have scoured the internet for anything relating to the area—of course, there is little information available from the most *accessible* sources. But I have found ways into certain... *databases*... of which even the most high-ranking federal officials are unaware. And this is only what I have discovered in relation to the valley. You can't fathom what knowledge I have found in the great, vast data expanse—information everywhere! We are only bound by our own minds! If you just devote yourself to searching! Seek and you will find! It's all *there*, waiting to be decrypted, discovered! Not merely the internet—beyond! The future! Creatures, dimensions, worlds unknown! *The future!*"

Mr V's speech halted. His stomach bulged and deflated as he bellowed massive amounts of air.

"Mr V?" Julian stood and stepped toward the man to help him, though there wasn't anything he could do. "Mr V, are you okay?"

Mr V's eyes bugged as he struggled for control. At last his breathing steadied. His face relaxed.

"I'm sorry, boy. I have... I have episodes. Even I become overloaded at times." He chuckled and smiled at Julian, warm, and more human than he had ever seemed. "You think I don't notice when your eyes glaze over? You are my superior in one thing. You are better able to stop the flow when it threatens to exceed your limits of stretching, when you might burst from new information."

"It's okay, Mr V. Don't talk. Just relax."

"Unfortunately, that defense mechanism has made you lazy. You can stretch more than you think. I will teach you. Yes, I will teach you. This, and many other things."

Mr V closed his eyes.

"The *future*," he whispered.

He began to snore.

Julian didn't know what to do. He was sure that his dad would be here soon, if he wasn't already waiting outside. But he didn't want to leave without Mr V letting him go—or without being paid.

"Mr V?" he half-whispered.

Should he shout? Should he jostle him awake? If a guy just passes out in the middle of conversation, especially one so fervent, wasn't sleep what he really needed the most?

Julian couldn't bring himself to touch him. Though leaving him this way carried its own risk, he decided it was the safest bet.

~

"How much today?" his dad said as he got in the car.

"Uh, I don't know. He just, like..." He was going to say *passed out*, but he realized that his dad would think the worst. He would want to go check on Mr V, and Julian really didn't want to go back in there. Especially with his dad. He hadn't thought until just now what his dad would think, walking in on him like that, naked and sweaty and swollen. It still made Julian uneasy and a little sick, even though he knew that Mr V was basically a nice guy. Dad would *definitely* freak out. Dads in general were bad about freaking out; Julian considered his especially prone to overreaction.

"He just... I guess he's in a weird mood. He kinda forgot, and I didn't want to bring it up."

"Son, I'm sure he meant to. You should go back in there and remind him."

"I don't want to bother him about it."

"Julian, it's not a bother, it's your job. He's an elderly man, he forgets things. He's not going to fault you for asking to be paid for your work. You need to be more assertive, you know, especially in a situation where it's clear he only—"

"Please, Dad, can we just go? I'll remind him on Monday."

His father held his gaze for a moment, then sighed. He shifted into gear and started driving.

"All right. I'm glad you're concerned about his feelings. But you really need to learn to be more confident."

"I know. I'll try. Monday, okay?"

His father tussled Julian's hair, something that really annoyed him lately. One second his parents are telling him to grow up, the next they're treating him like a little kid.

"I know where I want to go for my birthday next week."

"Oh yeah? What do you want? Calacino's? Gumbo's? You name it. We'll splurge."

"No, I mean, not to eat. I want to go to the dealership. I want to get my car, and then go take my test."

His dad's eyebrows raised. "Already? I mean, we can go to the DMV and get your license. But... just how much money do you *have*?"

"Well, I mean, not counting today's, I think..." He did a quick calculation. "Almost seventeen hundred? And today will easily put me over two thousand. And he's increased my pay. Well, once, at least. Yesterday I made five-seventy-five. So, like, if that keeps up, I should have a pretty big down payment."

"Whoa, son, hold on. Down payment? Remember what I said? Don't take out a loan, when you—"

A large pothole jarred the car violently. A new rattling developed underneath. He cursed under his breath and mumbled, "Can't afford another visit to the shop this month."

"See?" Julian said. "You always talk about how great it is to not have a payment. But how much do you spend every year to fix this piece of crap?"

His dad shrugged, his lips a tight line. Julian's excuse, though not completely honest regarding his own motivations, still held some logic to it. His dad couldn't deny it.

"This is exactly the reason I want a new car. Or at least, like, within the last *decade*. And you know I'll have the money. I don't have other expenses like you and Mom. I'll easily pay it off early. In fact, just today Mr V said I could keep working for him after the house is clean. Like, to keep things up and all, and feed him, and all that."

Julian watched his father's face. His eyes were fixed on the road, his knuckles were white—he often clutched hard at whatever was closest to him when he knew he was about to lose an argument. At last, he sighed.

"All right. I'll cosign. But you gotta promise me a few things, all right?"

"Anything, Dad. I really want a nice car."

"I understand that. But you have to be reasonable. Nothing that I can't insure."

"I'll even pay for insurance, if that's—"

His dad took one hand off the wheel and held it up. "Nothing unreasonable."

Julian slouched. He knew that his and his dad's ideas of *reasonable* tended to differ radically.

"Number two." The stiff palm transformed into bunny ears. "You don't flake out on this job. If you quit for any reason, you're in huge trouble. Because my credit will be on the line for this, you understand?"

"Don't worry, Dad."

"One last thing. No, make that the *first* thing. You will put *everything* in your paycheck toward the car until we're free and clear. *After* that, you will start saving for college. You can use some for fun stuff, and of course, you'll be buying gas and such. But you have to put a significant percentage of your money into savings."

This was more restrictive than he wanted. However, he didn't see another way around it. He nodded.

"Okay. Deal."

"I'm serious, Julian. The only reason I'm letting you do this is because you have a lot more money coming in than we expected, and you'll need to have a reliable car when you do go off to college."

"Dad, really. I'll be good for it. I'll be good for it all."

His father's brow relaxed. He smiled. "You're a good kid. I know you might think I'm being hard on you. I'm just trying to keep you out of trouble. I'm actually very proud of you."

"Thanks, Dad."

~

Julian hurried to his room before his sister or mother could sidetrack him. He shut and locked the door behind him, then took two huge steps across the floor to the phone on his nightstand.

No reply from Stacey.

Big surprise, he told himself. Still, he felt his happiness shrink in disappointment. She had seen the GIF, yet she hadn't even bothered to like it.

~

Still no word after dinner. He played Fortnite for a couple hours, which distracted him a little—but it couldn't conjure a message from Stacey. He smoothed out his hair, held his phone at what he hoped was the most flattering angle, and took a selfie. His heart lurched as soon as it sent.

He was being way too eager, when he wanted to be the cool, indifferent type of guy that she was usually seen with. He stared at his phone for a long five minutes without anything new happening.

This was torture.

He glanced at the book laying on his mattress's corner. Maybe if he read it this weekend, he would have a better idea of what Mr V was talking about all the time.

He turned off his phone, shut it in his sock drawer. Out of sight, out of mind, and all that. He lay down to read.

∞

"What are you doing?"

"Huh?"

His dad stood over him, his phone against his shoulder to muffle their conversation from whomever was on the other side. Julian could not tell whether his scrunched face meant worry or anger.

"Mr V is on the phone," he whispered. "He wants to know why you haven't come in to work. What do you want me to tell him?"

"Work? It's Saturday."

"Yes. I'm sure he knows that. You know that communication thing I told you about? You should try it sometime. In the meantime, I suggest you get ready."

I'm such an idiot.

His dad didn't work on Saturdays, so he had figured that was normal. He hadn't considered that Mr V might expect more attention. But why not? The man needed to eat, at the very least.

His dad walked away, apologizing for his son's tardiness, promising he would be there as soon as possible. Fortunately, Julian had been fully clothed when he nodded off. He ran to the bathroom, swearing at himself under his breath.

~

"I told him you forgot to set your alarm," his dad said as he drove up the mountain. "He didn't press me on why I hadn't noticed."

"Did he seem mad?" Julian wrung his hands. He had been doing so ever since he put on his seatbelt. All he could think about was getting fired. That pinprick of anguish became a marble between his shoulder blades. It orbited inside him at a glacial pace.

"I couldn't tell."

~

"Rip Van Winkle returns from the Catskills!"

Julian tried to swallow, but his throat was as dry as the dusty pages surrounding him. All the moisture in his body was fleeing out the pores on his forehead, the back of his neck, and his armpits.

"I'm really sorry, Mr V. I'm *really* sorry."

Mr V's face was blacked out by the fire behind him. Julian couldn't gauge how upset he was.

"You know, I was reading that book you lent me. I think I must have fallen asleep while I was reading."

"And what do you think so far?"

"Well, the thing with the sheep. I guess it's a robot? I mean, that's cool. I guess I don't understand why he's so obsessed, uh, with, like, having a real animal? Or why he has a robot animal in the first place? But I guess maybe I'll figure that out later on." He realized that he was speaking way too fast, but his nerves had taken over and he couldn't stop. "And the thing with adjusting his emotions and all. That was, like, pretty weird. I mean, I guess this is supposed to be in the future. Obviously, I mean. Robots and pushing a button to change your mood or something. Is he, like, talking about drugs or something? I guess I should say, I didn't get too far, since I fell asleep. I'm really sorry. I know I shouldn't have, it's a good book and all, I guess I was super tired, I don't know.

I'm really sorry for being late."

He finally closed his mouth. He felt the release of sweat from his jaw, heard the drops hit wood at his feet. The fireplace seemed brighter, hotter than normal. He squinted as his eyes struggled with the contrast.

Laughter burst from Mr V—Julian wouldn't say it sounded *friendly*, exactly, but it was better than the alternatives his imagination had predicted on the ride over. It carried on for several more seconds than he expected.

At last it faded. The blood rushing through Julian's ears sounded like waves breaking on a beach.

"You amuse me, son. I'm glad that you are reading, and that you are thinking about what you've read. But let's not be late again."

"Yes, sir."

"Very good. Before I forget: while I do expect you here on Saturdays—to clean, of course, but also because I need someone to make me lunch—I've decided to give you Sundays off, if you prefer. I take a fast on Sundays. Does that suit you?"

"Yeah, that sounds good."

"You might be tempted to assume that my fast is for religious purposes. Do you hold a faith of any particular persuasion?"

Julian shrugged. "I don't know. Christian, I guess. Mom was raised Catholic. Dad doesn't go to Mass though, so he doesn't make us go if we don't want. I go sometimes."

Mr V sniffed. "So, that would be a *no*. I do not say this in judgment, only to clarify. Faith is a driving force. Faith *changes* a person. You are a disciple of whomever—or *what*ever—in which your faith is directed."

Julian wished now that he hadn't been so non-committal. He hoped this wouldn't affect his pay.

"So, you're, like, a Christian then?"

"Now, I didn't say that. Actually, I didn't even say that *my* fasts were for religious reasons. I'm just curious about you. Christians are fascinating to me, but I do not subscribe to the core of their beliefs. I do not doubt that Yeshua the Nazarene performed many of the strange acts that his followers recorded. I am not, however, convinced of his identity."

"Huh? Yesh-who?"

"Joshua. *Jesus*, son. Jesus, an anglicized form of Iesous, which is the Greek rendering of the Hebrew name, Yeshua. Or, Joshua. Since he *was* Jewish, shouldn't we use the name he was born with?"

"Oh. Yeah, uh... I guess that makes sense."

"His followers say he is divine. A physical manifestation of Yahweh, Israelite god, the source of all things. That is what I do not agree with."

Julian felt uncomfortable talking to Mr V about religion. He opened his mouth, intending to suggest that he get to work—but Mr V was just getting started.

"Christians are funny, you know. They believe in what they call the *spiritual*, the *supernatural*. The word *supernatural* implies that which is not natural. I believe that all that is *true* is natural. So, I see this as a tacit distinction between what is *real*—true, natural—and what is *not* real—false, make-believe. They do not see it like this, of course. But I do. If anything *can* happen, then it *is* part of nature. However, there is much we do not understand about the nature of this universe—and others."

Julian nodded, but he was lost again. He had no way of knowing whether these ramblings proceeded from genius or senility.

"So, what the Christians mistake as divinity, I see as merely a hyper advancement of human nature. A man who was stretched, and stretched very far. To the point that he could overcome death."

Okay, this is definitely crazy, Julian thought.

But if Mr V had indeed gone insane—whether because of his solitude, or whatever sickness ailed him, or both—that did not mean he was dangerous. All the same, he really wanted to get out of this room, work, and get paid.

Unfortunately, it looks like the more time I spend in this room, the more I get paid.

"So, yes, I am a man of faith. Faith in infinite limits. In the unknowability of all that is possible. Faith in the improvement of the human species. Faith in all that is *natural*, even if that is not always what is *normal*. Do you understand?"

He didn't even try to fake it this time. "No, I'm sorry. I don't really get what you're saying."

Mr V sighed. "It is too soon. You are young. You have not seen enough. Learned enough. You've been raised to believe in very narrow limits to nature. But you'll see. In time, you'll discover how those assumed limits can be stretched."

He didn't know what to say to this. A bead of sweat trailed down from his hairline, past the corner of his eye, and settled on his cheekbone. He was intensely mindful of his need to ask about yesterday's pay, and about getting off for his birthday next Saturday. But now did not seem like a good time.

"Well, if that's all, Mr V, I should get started."

Mr V raised a hand. "Yes, yes. That is all."

~

After he finally got over his fear of losing his job, Julian let his mind fantasize about his new car and Stacey, and obsess over whether or not she had messaged him back, if she ever was going to. As he made his way down the hall, dusting picture frames and the occasional empty ceramic planter, he realized that, if he had really wanted to, he could have brought his phone and checked it in the telescope room.

Maybe next week. If he really needed to. For safety purposes.

No, maybe that was too risky. Even if Mr V couldn't see in that room, he might ask why Julian returned to it, if it was already clean. Especially if he did so multiple times.

Lunch came quickly—probably because he started late. But Mr V was no longer in his usual chatty mood. Without instruction, Julian scooped the eggs onto his boss's humongous belly—an act that had become surprisingly routine, as long as he didn't think about it too much. He backed away, stood at the door for twenty seconds, still curious about how the man ingested it all so quickly. But Mr V would not begin his meal with Julian watching.

He excused himself and resumed work.

~

At the moment Mr V's voice leaped from the speakers to call him back to the library, Julian was standing slack-jawed in the hall, face to weathered face with Ponce de León, empty ceramic eyes boring into his delicate flesh.

The conquistador's eroded gaze seemed to follow him as he left. That tight ache, currently focused on the small of his back, sank further inside, deepened, strained all within his chest cavity. A black hole imploding his center.

What is happening to me?

He wished there was some way to flip the switch on this pain, like in the novel Mr V had lent him. He worked up thoughts of home, his day off, family, the money, Stacey, the car—these did nothing.

~

Mr V remembered to pay him for both days without a reminder. Though Julian had suspected that his boss had been annoyed with him earlier, it didn't affect his wage very much. Seven hundred for Friday, and six-fifty for today. These astounding figures were emphasized when they appeared combined on the payment screen.

1,350 dollars for two days of work. And today I thought I was getting fired!

"Next Saturday is my birthday," he said, his confidence boosted.

"Well, congratulations, I suppose. When you've had as many birthdays as I, they tend to lose their novelty."

Mr V's lack of enthusiasm knocked Julian back a bit. Maybe asking for Saturday off would be too much. The man had to eat, after all. Except Sundays, for whatever reason. He hesitated, and Mr V filled the pause.

"I'm sorry, son. It's been a long time since my youth. I forget how exciting a new age can be to someone such as yourself. How old will you be?"

"Sixteen, sir."

"Sixteen! Well, now that *is* something. Something indeed. A milestone—at least I'm sure it will feel as such to you and your family. Well, good, I'll be sure to add a little extra gift to your paycheck next Saturday."

"Actually, sir, I meant to ask..."

"Well? Oh, I see. You intended to be absent, for celebratory purposes, most likely."

"Yeah. I wanted to go get my driver's license."

Mr V frowned and stared at the ceiling, on which the Horsehead Nebula was projected.

"Never mind. I mean, I'm sorry... I mean, you know. If it's too much to ask—"

"Nonsense!"

This exclamation was so loud and unexpected that Julian winced and stepped back.

"Nonsense, my boy! Sixteen! It took me some time, but I remember now. Sixteen. A licensed driver! In fact, this works out well for me. Since you'll be able to drive, I can send you occasionally for groceries and the like. Of course, I *would* get quite hungry if I was left alone for two days in a row. I propose a compromise: You come in for the morning, make me a good meal. A few other things, perhaps, if I think of them. Not many. Tell your father or mother to be back at 11:45. I promise I won't keep you a minute later."

"That's great," Julian said. He felt only somewhat disappointed—he would have liked to have the full day—but he would still have plenty of time to get his license, and the dealerships would likely be open until the evening. "Thank you, sir. Thanks for everything."

"It's nothing, my boy."

The nebula shifted, morphed. Folded.

"Now, one question for you, to keep your mind active over the weekend..."

Every time he breathed, he felt something sucking inside, like a leech was fastened to his heart.

∞

Julian could only stare at his phone. He had nearly given up.

But there it was! He didn't know what it meant. But it was acknowledgement, at least. Affirmation of his existence, if not of his desire.

Stacey had replied.

WHERE DID YOU GET THAT

He had no idea what she was talking about. The last thing he sent her was that selfie—seeing it again, his face flushed in embarrassment. The picture was focused incorrectly, with his messy sheets more defined than his face. How had he not fixed that before taking the shot? Yet it had not obscured his face enough to hide a large cowlick sticking out from the back of his head. When he took this picture, he thought he was cool. How? How had he believed that?

What was done was done. At least he had her attention.

what do you mean he replied.

Within seconds, those beautiful three dots appeared.

Then: **the book**

He checked the picture again. Just poking into frame was *Do Androids Dream of Electric Sheep?*.

borrowing it from my boss. You ever read it?

like five times. I love Phillip k dick

He started typing something else, then deleted it, unsure. She responded again.

listen I have to see that book

Julian was taken aback. If he had only known a lousy book would have gotten her attention, he would have tried to become a bookworm a long time ago.

Sure do you want to meet tomorrow?

He typed this but still did not believe it would come to anything, despite her apparent enthusiasm for this particular book.

can't tomorrow. You free tonight?

Was he free tonight? Hell yeah, he was free. What could possibly keep him away?

Even as he replied **sure what time, where?** the sickening realization of what *could* possibly keep him away darkened his mind, confirmed by her next message:

As soon as possible. I'm at work, will be open for another 45 min. You have a car, right?

There it was. The true demarcation between his world and hers. Forget high school social cliques, athleticism, grades, even differences in politics. There were men who drove, and boys who didn't. And he was exactly one week shy of obtaining that opener of worlds, that maker of men.

sure where do you work?

beckley library

Generally, he wouldn't even ask—neither of his parents would want to haul him all the way to Beckley this evening. True, that the library being his destination might encourage their help. However, by the time they got there, there would not be much time left for "studying" or whatever reason he could come up with.

Besides—having Mommy drop him off was the *last* way he wanted to make an impression with Stacey.

Preparing himself for defeat, he replied, **i don't know if i can make it in time**

ok. meet me at tudors? the one near lowes and chilis. ill buy your biscuit or whatever you want to eat just bring that book

Julian opened his window and stuck his head out, breathed in some fresh air, and checked his phone again.

Did Mr V do something to my head? Is this happening right now? Does this count as a date?

Her apparent desperation to meet had more to do with this book than with *him* exactly, so maybe this wasn't really a date. But a guy had to start somewhere, and he would take what he could get.

i'll bring the book but i can pay for my own food
Sounds good :D c u

He sighed, steadied himself. That cold hollow in his chest had not healed. He thought that if nothing else could fix his mood, this would.

If anything, it was worse.

Maybe the situation just hadn't settled in yet. When he saw her, this funk would surely disperse.

But he still had to get there. A ride from either of his parents was unlikely—and far from ideal.

He decided to get a Lyft to come pick him up. It would be a while before the driver arrived. In the meantime, he would take a shower, get some fresh clothes. Suddenly, he was acutely aware of Mr V's stink all over himself.

Yeah, gotta clean up for sure.

He let his parents know he was going to miss dinner. His mother protested, but his father saw something in his son's eye and defended his wishes with a softness that disarmed and convinced her.

~

Julian had the driver drop him off in front of Lowe's so that Stacey wouldn't see his pitiful, carless situation. He tried to appear relaxed on the short walk over to Tudor's Biscuit World, but his nerves and summer's humidity conspired against his sweat glands.

The fast-food breakfast place smelled like butter, salt, and cooking meat. Stacey sat in a booth in the back, tapping her foot. Their eyes met. She saw the book in his hand, smiled, and came to him. He swallowed.

"I remember you *now*," she said as they got in line. "Let me see it!"

She received the book from him. She frowned, not unhappily, but focused on the artifact. How she handled it reminded him of his father with his prized possession, a NCAA football signed by Major Harris in 1988. Whenever anyone new came to the house—even a UPS driver, once— he would wave them into the living room, beckon them with hushed tones, lift it delicately from its kicking tee. Hardly ever taking his eyes from the leather, he would extend it with both hands for his guests to admire and touch—only with their fingertips—then he would snatch it away and return it to the shelf.

She lifted the front cover gingerly and peered at the copyright page. "It is. It really is," she whispered.

A gray-haired man in khakis and a button-up shirt cleared his throat behind them. They were holding up the line.

"Sorry," Julian said. "I'll get a country ham and egg biscuit. And a water. What do you want, Stacey?"

She finally looked up. "Oh, uh. Just a sweet tea for me."

"You sure? I'm buying."

She had already returned her attention to the book. He shrugged and nodded to the cashier. He paid and took their number to the table.

"You not hungry?"

She flipped a few pages in the book. "Do you know what this is?"

"Yeah, I mean... I haven't finished it yet. It's science fiction though, I guess. Oh..." His face reddened. "Right, you knew that already."

"This is a first edition. A first edition hardcover."

"Yeah? I didn't know that. It makes sense, though. Mr V's

got a pretty big library. He let me borrow it. First edition, that's pretty cool."

She wiped a spot on the table that did not seem dirty to Julian, set a new napkin there, and placed the book on it. She started to type something on her phone.

The waiter came with his biscuit and the drinks. Stacey looked up from her phone to make sure the cup of iced tea was an acceptable distance from the book.

"So is it, like, rare or something?" He took a bite of his biscuit. It burned the inside of his mouth, but he didn't dare spit it out in front of her. He chewed quickly and drowned the pain with his water.

She shoved the phone in his face. He saw thumbnails of the book's cover alongside listings priced from a couple thousand dollars to fifteen grand.

"Holy shit."

She smirked. "Yeah. You said your boss just let you *borrow* it?"

"Yeah. I didn't realize, though. Dude. Fifteen thousand dollars. That's..." His appetite waned as he understood his carelessness. This was a way bigger deal than a Major Harris autographed football.

"Yeah. I can't believe I was so stupid to suggest meeting you here. All this grease. I'm sorry. It was just the first place that came to my head."

He stared in shame at his fingers, shining from handling his biscuit sandwich. Now he realized why she had only asked for tea.

"Yeah, I'll definitely wash my hands before I take that back."

"So, who did you say you worked for again? I need to meet this guy."

"You know that creepy-ass mansion up in High Point?"

"I don't think I've ever been through High Point."

"Actually, I never did until I got this job, now that I think of it. Though I knew about Mr V, somehow. I guess you hear stuff, you know."

"Mr V?"

"Yeah, that's the old dude who lives there. He's, uh…"

Flames in his mind's eye. Darkness, then the glow of a projector. Smooth, tight, white flesh. A snake dangling underneath.

"He's sick. I clean and, like, cook his meals and stuff."

"Aw, that's so sweet of you."

"Well, he pays me pretty good."

"Yeah?"

"Yeah…"

He stopped himself from getting too specific. He got the feeling now that the money would not impress her as much as he had imagined, and he didn't want her realizing how mercenary his motives truly were.

"You should see his library, though."

Her eyes widened. She crossed her arms, leaned forward with her elbows propped on the table. "I would *love* to see it. Do you think he would let me?"

Julian swallowed. He glanced down and couldn't help but notice her breasts, squeezed within the square formed by her arms. He forced his gaze to his biscuit, wondering for a moment if she had noticed the delay in where his eyes had rested.

Mr V was big on privacy—well, his own, at least. There was no way he would be comfortable with Julian bringing a visitor to gape at his mansion.

More than that, the idea of Stacey seeing the fat, sick man made his stomach turn, though he couldn't say why. Perhaps a part of him feared that she would think Mr V's disease had somehow infected him.

He met her eyes again. The pupils were wide within their soft, periwinkle rings. These two polished bits of unearthly black stones hitched up his breath like the frigid, obsidian marble lodged in his chest.

~

"Okay, you turn up this way. Yeah. This is it."

Stacey shifted down as the tight turn steepened. Julian was both in awe of and shamed by her familiarity with her Jeep's manual transmission. The suspension creaked as potholes jostled the vehicle, but it felt natural, it felt right. As the vehicle opened its gullet and chugged down the stream of bad road, Stacey's shoulders hung loose, her left hand's grip on the wheel stayed relaxed, her right wrist rested limply on the stick. In that moment, Julian saw that she was not a sports car kind of girl. He had been a fool to even dream it. He had known nothing of her, and probably knew nothing about women in general.

"So, like, you work at the library, huh?"

She scowled. "Yeah, so what?"

He shrugged. "No, I mean, it's cool. I wasn't making fun of you or anything."

"Sorry. I didn't mean to get defensive. It's just... my dad gives me a hard time about stuff. I don't know. Doesn't think I should care so much about my grades like I do. Doesn't think I should go to college. It's weird. It's like he thinks a girl should be pretty but not smart."

"That's crazy," he said. His ears burned. He had no grudge against Stacey going to college, but his superficial assumptions about her identity had been uncomfortably similar.

"Yeah, I don't get it. We used to be really close, when I was a little girl. Then Mom left him for some engineer in Morgantown and he started drinking a lot more and started... well, he kind of turned into an asshole. As if Mom hadn't abandoned me too, you know? But whatever." She turned and glared at him. "Don't you dare tell him about my job. He thinks I'm a part of a summer cheerleading program."

He put his hands up. "Don't worry. I've never even met him."

Stacey relaxed. She smiled sheepishly and turned back to the road. "Sorry. Doing it again. It's better if I just don't think about it. Maybe that's why I like books so much."

"Oh!" Julian pointed ahead. "There's his driveway, see it?"

She nodded and pulled in. The house grew large and dark against the low evening sun, and his anxiety rose with it. How had he agreed to this?

"Okay, listen," he said as Stacey parked. His armpits gushed as if a spring had opened inside them. "Mr V... he's like... I don't know how to explain it. He's sick. And kind of cranky. You know, I'm not sure this is a great idea."

"Relax. I don't have to meet the guy. I just want to see his library. We can peek in the window, right?"

"Yeah, but—"

Stacey stepped out of the Jeep. Julian closed his eyes and cursed himself before removing his seatbelt and hurrying to catch her before she started across the lawn.

"The dude's got cameras," he whispered. "Like, everywhere. He's super paranoid."

"Really? Why?" She didn't stop, but she stooped lower, making a show of stealth to appease him.

She thinks this is funny.

Julian sighed. He followed her. She pressed her back up against the brick and giggled. He leaned next to her. The wall was slippery against him.

"Okay, chief," she whispered. "Where's the library?"

"All the way on the corner this way. The windows are big. But he's always in there, so don't just stand in the window and stare. If he hasn't seen us yet, he'll see us through the windows if we're not careful."

She made her way along the wall, crawling beneath each window. Julian did the same. Even though he knew Mr V was in the library, he didn't want to take the chance that any cameras in the halls or other rooms caught their figures sneaking past.

He tapped her on the shoulder when they got to the library. She nodded. Her eyes were bright. He ached for all his ignorant preconceptions; he had treated her like an unapproachable deity instead of a normal human being. She was more—not less—than his fantastical ideal, that fiction which he now saw as utterly absurd, even demeaning. He had worshiped a cartoon, not a person. He disgusted himself.

She ducked beneath the window. Squatting, she glanced at Julian. He wanted to stop her, but her smile paralyzed him. She rose.

"Shit." She dropped.

"What? Did he see you? Oh man, if—"

"No, chill out dude. It's just, he's got really thick curtains."

"Oh yeah. I forgot about those." He wiped his sweaty hands against his shirt. "Well, I guess we better go."

But she was already back up, cupping her face against the glass. "There's, like, barely even a gap to see through. It's super dark. Looks like there's a fire. Who has their fireplace going this time of year?"

"I don't know. I told you. He's got, like, some kind of disease or something."

"You sure he's in here?"

"You know, maybe not. Maybe he's in another room. You don't see anything on the ceiling, do you?"

"There's hardly any light in there. Just the fireplace."

So, he wasn't watching the cameras, at least. This calmed Julian somewhat, but he still felt uneasy.

"You were right, I can't see much but looks like tons of books in there. So awesome. What's that... what the—"

She turned for a moment to Julian with her eyes wide, then squinted into the glass.

"Come on, let's get out of here." He grabbed her arm.

"What's with you?" She probably meant to sound annoyed, but her face looked pale, almost green, and her voice quavered.

"I just feel weird about this now. You know? Like, he's a

sick dude. We shouldn't be spying on him."

"Yeah. Yeah, okay."

~

Stacey was distant. Julian knew he had ruined whatever rapport they had as quickly as he had built it. He did not know how to salvage the relationship. He let her drive him all the way back to Beckley rather than admit that he in fact did not have a car parked in the Tudor's parking lot.

And yet, despite his awkward shame, he still preferred more time in her presence.

"Sorry you didn't see much."

Of course this was a lie, but how else to cut through the curtain that had formed between them, thick as those velvet drapes in Mr V's library?

She shrugged after a few seconds. "Yeah," she said, then muttered something else.

"What was that?"

She looked at him, blinked. Looked back at the twisting two-lane. "Yeah. Yeah, didn't see anything."

A throb in his center—that pulsing dark matter.

"There was like... I thought I saw like a really big globe or something in there. A big round thing. But it looked blank. Maybe white? Maybe orange? The fire..."

Julian squirmed. "I don't... yeah I guess maybe he's got a globe or something in there. I don't really pay attention. I mean, hard to notice anything when there's all those books, right?" He conjured a weak laugh. "Who knows what that old man's got."

"Yeah. I guess. I just thought it like—"

Momentum yanked his head and arms forward, but his seatbelt locked against his torso and kept him from hitting the dashboard. The Jeep's tires skidded. They came to a full stop just as three doe finished bounding across the road in the twilight.

"Whew," Julian said. "Close one."

"It was moving."

"What, the deer?"

She shook her head slowly. "The giant white globe."

"Maybe a window was open somewhere we didn't see. Maybe a breeze turned it. Globes spin, right?"

"Not like that. It was growing. And shrinking. Up and down. Like a fish's gill when you have it out of the water too long and it's trying to gulp up oxygen from the air and it can't get enough. A big, shiny, white balloon swelling and deflating. Over and over."

She started driving again.

"And there was something... something else..."

Julian did not know anything else he could say to dismiss what she had seen. The dark place inside of him swelled like Mr V's stomach. Stacey's expression made him wonder if a black ball had begun to grow within her ribs as well.

∞

He lay in bed all Sunday morning, waiting for Stacey to message him, wondering how much she had seen that she couldn't bring herself to say, wondering if last evening had made everything he had done so far pointless. She was disgusted with him now—probably assumed that Mr V's sickness was contagious, that Julian had it, and maybe she had it, too.

His stomach turned. How did he know that Mr V's sickness *wasn't* contagious? Why had he given that possibility so little thought? His throat constricted. He reached for Phillip K. Dick as a distraction, but after fifteen minutes of his eyes running up and down the same two paragraphs, he gave up.

Carmen knocked on his door. "Will you make lunch for me?"

"What is Dad doing?"

"He said to ask you. He says he is sick and trying to sleep. And Mom isn't back yet and I'm hungry."

"What's wrong with Dad?"

"I don't know. He's snoring now."

Just a cold or something. I would have known by now if Mr

V's problems were contagious. Dad wouldn't show symptoms before me.

His stomach was so clenched in anxiety that he didn't think it would keep lunch down, but he might as well fix it for his sister.

"Okay, fine. I'll be out in a second."

Carmen's smile faded as Julian set her lunch on the table. "Ew."

"What? You like eggs, right?"

"Um, no. Well, maybe. But not that much, doofus. It looks gross."

"Don't say 'doofus,'" he said. His gaze trickled down the steaming, yellow heap of cooked embryonic matter. He had fixed the same lunch Mr V always ordered, inconsiderate of how inappropriate the serving size was for his little sister—or for any normal person.

"You don't have to eat them all. Here's another plate. Just scoop off what you want."

She shot him a sideways look. "You're weird." She mined two eggs worth from the yellow mountain and slid them onto her plate. "Can I get some ketchup?"

"Yeah, yeah. Sorry."

He took a half-empty bottle of ketchup from the fridge. As he slapped its bottom and squirted it over the plate, saliva gathered under his tongue.

"That's too much!"

He released his grip on the bottle. The eggs were fully coated in scarlet goo.

"Sorry."

She pushed away the plate. A glob of ketchup escaped from its edge and left a trail on the table. "I'll wait for Mom to get home," she said, and left.

He dropped into her vacated seat. The eggs were too sweet, but they slid down easily enough, given their added lubrication.

His hunger surprised him. Suddenly, he was starving. He no longer worried about puking. The remainder of the egg heap went down fine.

∞

He did not sleep well. An hour before sunrise, he released his phone from the charger and slunk to the kitchen for coffee. His dad had already got it ready so that all he had to do was press the button. The carafe's black belly fed from the thin brown stream. He watched, not quite lucid.

Sputter, koosh. Drip.

It seemed that the carafe summoned the brown line into itself with its own gravity, a sucking force that did not match the earth's. Too fast—or too slow? Or was the thread of coffee rising back into the machine? No, no. The dark liquid filled the pot steadily. He could see it climbing the white marks printed on the outside of the glass.

The continuing trickle brought to mind a pressure in his bladder that he hadn't noticed. He acknowledged his discomfort but remained hunched in front of the ten-dollar plastic auto-drip.

Trickle, drip, gurgle. Sputter, koosh.

The machine beeped. He lifted the carafe of sloshing darkness from its hot, wet cave. Poured into his father's favorite Mountaineers mug.

Warmth, relief.

He looked down at his leg, his boxers. At first, he thought he had spilled the coffee.

"Uuunh."

He left the mug and hobbled to his room for clean underwear. His mind operating at the lowest of wakeful levels, he was conscious of shame, and itchy moisture in his crotch, and a dull ache somewhere between his throat and stomach, but he could not articulate a thought. He was a mobile, unintelligent mass of pain.

~

"You okay, Booger?"

"What? Yeah, fine."

"Why don't you drive? I can pull over if you want. Don't you need more supervised hours or something?"

"I got them all."

"What was that? Don't mumble."

"I said I got them all. Just need to take the test."

"Oh. Well, I thought you still would want to. Buying a car is all you ever talk about. You know, once you get your own, I'm not going to chauffeur you around in it. You gotta do that yourself. Part of the deal, Booger."

"I just don't feel like it, okay?"

Carmen, who had to ride with Julian and his mom every morning so that she wasn't left alone, said something that he didn't hear. His hand slipped into his pocket, and his fingers wrapped gently around his phone.

He had messaged Stacey while waiting for them to get dressed. Those awful, hope-inducing three dots had appeared—disappeared—appeared—vanished, nothing.

When his mother had yelled that they were ready, he had pocketed the phone without thinking.

"You've been just so spacey lately. Teenager stuff, I guess."

"Yeah. I guess."

"You know I love you, right?"

It was all he could do not to check his messages. Amazingly, his parents seemed pleased by Mr V's strict no-phones policy. If his mom saw that he had it, she would probably make him leave it in the car.

"Right?"

"Yeah. I know." He removed his hand from his pocket. "I love you too."

"Don't mumble, Booger."

"Please don't call me that."

"Booger!" Carmen screamed. She laughed.

~

The mansion's red brick was darker somehow, like blood that had gone stale and crusty. Julian glanced at the sky, expecting cloud cover, but there was none. He felt sick. His mother blew him a kiss and drove away.

He entered, consciously keeping his hands in view as he walked to the library.

"The eggs." Mr V sounded agitated.

Julian closed his eyes.

Shit.

"Don't tell me you forgot them."

"I, uh—"

"I'm *ravenous.*"

He hung his head and endured a long silence. He touched the corner of his eye and found it moist.

"All right. Well, your mother has left, so there's nothing else to do about it today. This will be reflected in your payment."

Julian nodded.

"Well, go on then. Get to work."

"Yes, sir."

He cleaned in a fog of gloom and anxiety. The pressure and heat in the dusty upstairs hallways were incongruous with its darkness. Sweat poured off of him. Mucus gathered in the back of his throat and dripped down into his lungs. He coughed constantly. He suspected that he was doing more to contaminate these rooms than improve them.

Stacey had seen *something* through that window. But

what could have spooked her so badly? Mr V laying on the table? A gruesome sight, maybe. Had she mistaken him for something worse than a swollen, pasty, diseased old man? Surely Mr V wasn't *that* terrifying.

Julian felt a sharp pain behind his breastbone. He grabbed his chest. A flash of terror, images of himself collapsing from a heart attack—fifteen was too young to die like that. Heartburn from the coffee? Wasn't fifteen too young for heartburn, too?

Another sensation halted these thoughts: a short vibration against his right thigh. His hand shot into his pocket on reflex; he barely managed to keep from retrieving its contents. He looked into the corner of the ceiling where, sure enough, a camera was angled directly at him. He stared at it too long, a deer enchanted by the lights of its imminent demise.

There was nothing to do but his job. He bent over a shelf and sprayed a thick layer of wood polish. The chemical-lemon scent went to his head. He stepped back for a deep breath, which initiated a tickle in his lungs and a coughing fit to clear them.

Stacey messaged me. It's her; it's gotta be.

The black knot tightened inside. He tried to release its pressure in a long moan from low in his throat.

Maybe she had gotten busy, and that's why it took so long to hear from her. Maybe she wanted to meet up again. Maybe she had not seen anything in Mr V's office. Maybe... well, what the hell did Julian know about the female mind? Maybe he had misread her face that night, misread her harsh silence.

He knew he could do nothing until he saw her message. He also knew that he was on thin ice with his boss. Mr V was in a mood. Mr V was hungry.

There was only one room in this vast house where Julian was sure of his privacy: the room with the telescope and the malfunctioning camera. He picked up a spray bottle on a thin pretense of having missed a spot last week, hoping desperately that Mr V had busied himself in some obscure occult or philosophical internet forum and would not ask him why he was returning to that room.

His pulse surged mightily and did not recede when he at last closed himself within the room's solitude.

Something was different here. The room seemed emptier than the last time.

He fumbled with his phone; it dropped and clattered across the floor, resting on the same spot where the brown glass paperweight had shattered last week.

"No!" The word escaped from him involuntarily. He froze for a few seconds, but nothing came from the intercom. His legs cleared the length of the room quickly and without a sound. At his feet was the phone, staring back up into Julian's twisted face with its black camera eye.

Juan Ponce de León's blank, terra cotta gaze came to mind. Hadn't there been a statue in this room before? But his worries were too urgent to dwell on this.

He squatted, palmed the phone, turned it over. Radial web-like cracks transformed the screen into a kaleidoscope.

"No, no, no, no."

He frantically swiped his thumb back and forth across the jagged ridges. The little bubble of Stacey's picture and that mocking red number in its corner stuttered. Red smears appeared on the screen, followed by crimson traces settling into the glass's innumerable fault lines. At last, he managed to open her messages:

i dont know what kind of sick joke you are trying to pull on me but it is sick and stop talking to me please

i don't konw how you did it and what you even did or if that weird man is in on it or you are just taking advantage of access to his house and he is gone or what but i know that it wasn't real what was in there and i dont know if you wanted to scare me or disgust me or make me think your some kind of badass or what but that's not what i'm about and now I can't get that out of my head and it's making me

sick. **DON'T TRY TO CONTACT ME EVER AGAIN.**
I am blocking you now.

Another moan discharged from his throat, without catharsis. The finality and severity of her words weakened his legs. He sat on the floor and stared at the messages hiding behind the cracked glass and veneer of drying blood.

The pit inside him felt the size of a melon rather than the walnut it had been. Incoherence threatened its return. He gritted his teeth.

"Come to the library."

He looked up to the camera. Was it the same one as before? The possibility—no, the *probability*—that Mr V had hired someone to fix the malfunctioning camera some evening after Julian had discovered it had never crossed his mind until now, and the weight of this realization struck him with malice.

But there was still the chance—the hope—that Mr V saw nothing. He may have called on him for the very reason that he could not see him on his screen. Or maybe there was some other reason.

"Julian? The library. Bring a bucket of hot water and a sponge. And a fresh towel."

And there it was. Something in the library needed a sponge. Somewhat encouraged, though still reeling from Stacey's rejection, he returned the phone to his pocket, wiped his eyes and nose on his shoulder, and soldiered to one of the cleaning closets. His feet became sacks of gravel on the way.

~

Hot putrescence nearly leveled him. He considered that the weekend may have recalibrated his senses so that he was no longer as resistant to Mr V's smell—but this seemed at an intensity even greater than the first day.

The doors shut him in the library like a mausoleum vault. The fire burned brighter than ever behind Mr V's silhouette, but the room was somehow darker than normal. Steam creeped from the bucket up his right forearm like some kind of dank spirit. The towel over his left shoulder slipped a little, and he had to cock his torso at an awkward angle to keep it from falling.

"Come to me. Set the bucket near the foot of my table."

The hot water splashed him as he lugged it forward. His shorts clung to his thigh as a second, stiflingly moist skin. When he finally set it down and raised his eyes to Mr V's swell, he wondered at its size—surely even the most malignant of tumors could not grow as quickly as Mr V's belly had. The man's head was hidden by it; his arms and legs seemed like the stumpy plastic limbs of a doll attached to this incomprehensible flesh-mountain.

Though he had reason enough to believe that his cell phone usage had gone undiscovered, Julian's nerves were dialed high, and the miserable sucking pit inside him throbbed in a slower, torturous undulation.

"I suppose you may have guessed what I require. I understand your natural revulsion, and I do not take offense. My distaste for it is greater than yours, believe it or not. Alas, it comes with my situation, and is one of your duties."

Julian blinked, processing Mr V's intention. He looked down at the bucket and sponge, then back at the mountaintop, which was higher than his extended hands could reach.

"You'll be careful around my head, I'm sure. That area is especially sensitive. Start there. Then my arms and legs, then finish with my torso. Do not be shy with the sponge after you finish with my face. Scrub good and hard, then dry with the towel. It is a bit of effort, but it is quite simple, and you'll be done in no time."

Julian silently dry heaved three times. Fortunately, this involuntary response was sheltered from Mr V's view.

"Well, come on, then. Leave the bucket there. Wring the sponge out good, first. Keep it away from the equipment near my head. Be careful you don't splash or knock the bucket over there, either. The computers on that side are not as close to me, but they are no less immune to moisture's destructive properties."

Julian steadied himself, soaked the sponge, and wrung it out above the bucket. The sponge dripped—one, two—he stared hard. The droplets—

Falling, not rising. Falling, not rising.

He found it difficult to meet Mr V's eyes. His throat felt thick and his stomach shriveled.

"Wrap the towel around the sides and bottom of my head, so that the water does not drip down my cable housing and ruin things."

"Huh?"

Mr V lifted his head an inch. Underneath, he saw a thin cushion, with a baseball-sized hole in its center. A thick metal cable protruded from the back of Mr V's head and was threaded through it. This was the whipping, snake-like creature that Julian had before spied beneath the prostrate old man.

He applied the towel as Mr V instructed. Their eyes met for a moment. He quickly looked away.

"I thought you would have picked up on this by now," Mr V said as he nestled his head into a comfortable position within the towel. "Do you ever see me with a mouse? A keyboard? I control it all this way. With a thought. An electrical signal straight from my brain shoots down the wires into my computers."

He applied the sponge to Mr V's bald pate.

"You're not, though—I mean, you're still..."

"Well? Speak your words, boy."

He licked salty sweat from his upper lip, tried to manufacture some saliva, swallowed. "Like, in the book..."

"Oh, a machine?" He chuckled. "An android? Well, now that is amusing. No. In fact, this is not even as invasive as it appears. Unfortunately, a projection screen is still required, as you've seen. For now, data is only traveling one way—brain to the computers, you see. I do not trust output feed from the internet as input into my mind."

Julian wiped the sponge carefully around Mr V's face. Water seeped into the corners of the old man's mouth. He sputtered and blew. His spit coated Julian's forearm.

"This super-direct interface is experimental, obviously. Who knows what a straight pipeline from the internet into my thoughts would do, without the filter of sight? Perhaps in a decade or two, I'll work out something I can trust. Stretching, always stretching. Becoming. But do not be careless. Stretch too quickly, and one might snap."

Julian concentrated on keeping a steady, gentle hand with the sponge, and not getting water into the man's orifices or eyes. At last he finished with the head and neck—what little neck there was. The man no longer even had shoulders and a chest. Just one massive balloon.

He removed the towel and returned to the bucket. As he dunked the sponge, he saw that his hand was shaking.

His senses had not grown used to the heat and smell. He felt himself about to puke. Without thinking, he knelt, grabbed the rim of the bucket, and hung his head over the hot water.

Thankfully, it was only another round of painful dry heaving. Tears shot from his ducts; sweat streamed from his temples. All into the bucket, where it mingled with the water and Mr V's sponge-juice and became one funky stew. Thinking of this brought another convulsion which did raise some acid to his mouth, but he swallowed it to keep the water—well, *clean* wasn't the word, but he could think of no other.

The fire seemed to intensify. Julian struggled to find his composure. The miserable, throbbing black hole inside his chest had bloated, affecting his shoulders, his stomach, his spine. He could not understand this anguish. He could not understand Stacey's message. He could not understand anything.

He stood. At least he did not have to look into Mr V's face

again. And Mr V could not see his. Tears came steadily as he scrubbed the limbs. He hoped that Mr V would mistake the drops that fell on him for water from the sponge.

Was that movement in the corner of the room? Something solid waiting eagerly in the shadows? A tall figure adjusting his weight from one heel to another?

No, it was the fire throwing long shades to dance across the books.

What did she think she saw in here? There's nothing! Nothing but a sick old dude!

He ran the sponge up and down Mr V's left thigh, careful not to disturb his boss's only covering: the cloth that contained the small region between his legs and his belly. Would he have to clean that, too?

It must have been me. I must have done something. She knew I was freaking out. I freaked her out, too.

The car was his only hope—or was that all worthless, too? He had thought he knew what would impress her, but Stacey had pulled up those assumptions like they were a whole lot of weeds infesting the garden of his worldview. He was wrong about nearly everything.

The left foot, then the next leg. Mr V was surprisingly quiet. There, in another corner—again, long shadows creeped.

He would message her when he got home. What would he say? Could he fix this?

His sponge caught the edge of Mr V's groin-towel. He pulled back, but it was too late. The cloth slipped from Mr V's skin.

He could not help from staring at what had been hidden—or what hadn't. No genitals of any kind to see. No pubic hair, not even any kind of post-surgery scar. A smooth joining between the legs. Nothing more.

"Ah, well, yes," said Mr V. "We were going there eventually, my boy. What is sex? Weakness. Distraction. A biological drive which dulls the intellect. An unfortunate necessity of your current genetic makeup. It causes the most grotesquely irrational behavior. What could you be? Do you ever wonder? What could you be *without* that foolish girl obfuscating your mind?"

Stacey—how could he *not* think of her? Her carefree smile. The way her blue eyes met his without any amount of self-doubt or deference. And, of course, her sublime curves.

Then, a realization:

He saw us.

Mr V chuckled. "Sure, I know. Saturday night. The phone today. My boy, what has she *done* to you?"

Julian thought there was a disturbance behind him in the stifling air—a breeze through the window? But the windows were closed.

"Without sex—think of it, if only you could—without that drive, just *imagine*. I said it was a necessity—for you, for nearly everyone in the human race, *such as it exists currently*."

Julian's every pore seeped foulness. He sobbed, unsure of why, unsure of this place, unsure of Mr V, unsure of everything.

"But what is it I always say? Humans are capable of greatness—if willing to *become*. If willing to *evolve*. If willing to *stretch*."

With this Julian imagined that the already massive belly next to him grew an inch—another trick of the flames!

"Now, for the rest of me."

Julian did not know how Mr V expected him to get all of it. He circled, reaching as far as he could. Mr V muttered more about the usual things—adaptation, the stars, dimensions of esoteric knowledge untapped by modern science and dominant religions. Julian felt every syllable through his sponge as he polished the tight, white dome's base. His thoughts steadily lost coherence. His anxiety inflated and consumed him.

"For the rest, you must climb."

He lifted himself onto the table easily enough. He stood

between the thighs. The belly had been insurmountable enough before. Now it was wet.

Julian placed his bare hand on the mountain, skin-on-skin for the first time. A nearly electric sensation.

The belly did something—changed... *flexed*... indentations formed. Steps for the pilgrim to ascend.

They were placed so that he needed both hands and feet. He held the salty, bitter sponge in his teeth.

He climbed. Fully saturated in his own sweat, all of his clothes clung to his body like oppressive demons attached to a host. His foot slipped from one of the holds, and for a moment, he thought he was going to go sliding all the way down. But he leaned in and kept his grip.

The air near the top was nearly impossible to breathe. His lungs churned. His heart beat faster than it ever had. He despised his contact with the belly, but what was there to do? He was so high up, and there was such a great chance of falling. He flattened against the dome and wriggled to its center. He risked his security and rose to a knees-and-elbows position. He surveyed the room from his roost. Everything he saw below him wobbled.

Shadows slithered in the corners—the fire—the growing belly—

Nothing! Tricks! Imagination!

Tears and sweat, hot on the cheeks—stars swirled above—from the projector? Yet the bulb was dark, darker than night—

Where is the ceiling?

He wept on the mound, and with his sponge, he smeared his tears on its skin.

"You remember what I said." The words resounded from a cavern beneath his knees.

Terra cotta soldiers emerged below him into undeniable view. Julian gasped. He choked on mucous.

"I don't understand! I don't know what's going on!"

"I meant to guide you—what greatness you could have

become! You seemed so close. So perceptible. So teachable."

"I'm sorry! I'm sorry I brought the phone, okay? I'm sorry!" He dropped the sponge. It fell—fell—fell—it did not rise, though time seemed to play and reverse, play and reverse—so far below, into the fire!

How was the fire so far below?

"Why is it so dark up here?" He panted, his lungs burning for oxygen. "It's so hot! It's so hot up here with the stars!"

The voice, from beneath: "It was never about the phone, boy. You brought *her* here. She witnessed things most humans will *never* be ready for. How was I such a fool to think you were nearly ready?"

"I'm ready! Just tell me what I need to know. I don't know anything anymore! How could I?"

The skin slackened—was the mountain deflating? Not exactly. Around him rose a circular white ridge. He tried to stand and make a break for the edge—his foot turned on pliable ground. He fell onto his backside and grabbed for his ankle. It had been swallowed, like it was mired in clay.

He screamed. He cried. He pounded his fists, and they stuck. His buttocks sank; the flesh-walls rose.

On the crater's surrounding ridge appeared four terra cotta spectators with blank, weathered stares.

There was nothing else but the flesh below; ash and swirling stars above.

He sank.

AUTHOR'S NOTE

Thanks for reading this new edition of *Unknowing, I Sink*. I would love to hear what you thought of it. If you go to my website, tghuguenin.com, you can find out how to contact me directly. If you are interested in keeping up with my latest releases, there you will also see a link to sign up for my email newsletter.

There's a reason why so many independent authors keep asking readers to review their books—it really helps us out! Those who have never heard of us need a gentle nudge from our fans to click that *Buy* button. So please—a little review goes a long way. If you liked this book, please review it.

I'm so glad you found my strange little story, and I hope you enjoyed it. Thanks for reading and reviewing.

Stay in touch!

— Timothy G. Huguenin
Elkins, WV
2022

Timothy G. Huguenin is a hillbilly writer of the strange and spooky, living in the dark Allegheny Mountains of West Virginia. He is the author of *When the Watcher Shakes*, *Little One*, and *Unknowing, I Sink*. His short fiction has appeared in publications including *Vastarien: A Literary Journal*, *Dim Shores Presents Vol. 2*, and *Anthology of Appalachian Writers Vol. XI*. Find out more about his writing and get a free e-book by visiting tghuguenin.com.

CHECK OUT THESE OTHER BOOKS!

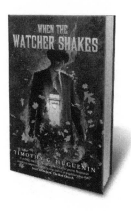

WEST VIRGINIA AUTHOR PROJECT 2021
ADULT FICTION WINNER

The walls were meant to keep evil out—
but they only hid the evil within.

John has given up his ordinary life to find wisdom traveling the country and enjoy the freedom of living as a nomad. But when he stumbles across a mysterious town tucked away in the Appalachian Mountains, walled off from modern society, he discovers a group of people who could use some freedom of their own. Are they a harmless religious sect, or is there something malignant beneath the surface?

"A chilling entry in the small-town horror genre. Huguenin combines suspense, mystery, and action in page-turning style." — Scott Nicholson, *The Red Church*

Death is cold.

Kelsea Stone can't remember her childhood, and frankly, she doesn't really care. She's doing fine on her own in L.A. without any family to tie her down. But when she finds out her estranged birth parents have died and left her their house in Canaan Valley, West Virginia, she discovers more than just an inheritance waiting for her in the mountains. An angry presence lingers there, and it won't rest until it has had its revenge.

"The heart-racing mystery will keep readers wondering who to trust and how the story will end." — *Publishers Weekly*

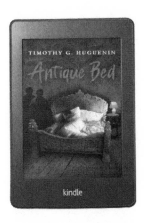

As kids we always used to say that the old hardware building was haunted. I don't believe it no more—at least I don't think so.

In desperate need of housing after her boyfriend dumps her, Sandy finds an apartment in Augustus Valley for a price she can hardly believe. There are rumors that the place is haunted, but she knows that's all nonsense. Sure, the building is old and has its quirks—but it's a killer deal.

Antique Bed: A Horror Novelette is a shorter work that should take between thirty and forty minutes to read... But this disturbing tale will stick with you long after.

Download *Antique Bed* for FREE at tghuguenin.com

Made in the USA
Columbia, SC
25 September 2022

67591251R00057